How Raven Got His Crooked Nose

An Alaskan Dena'ina Fable

Retold by
Barbara J. Atwater and Ethan J. Atwater

Illustrated by Mindy Dwyer

ALASKA
NORTHWEST
BOOKS®

"Slow down, child," said Grandmother. "It is better to take your time and do things right. Do you know the story of how *Chulyen* the raven got his crooked nose?"

Chulyen (CHOOL yen)

Granddaughter shook her head.

"No? Then sit and I will tell you a *sukdu*."

sukdu (SOOK du): story

Once, Chulyen had a very straight nose. He thought it was quite handsome. He was able to do many things with his straight nose.

But Chulyen was a trickster and sometimes he did things that were not wise. Sometimes they got him in trouble.

"But how did Chulyen lose his nose?" asked Granddaughter.

"He would never say, my dear. Maybe he was too embarrassed," answered Grandmother.

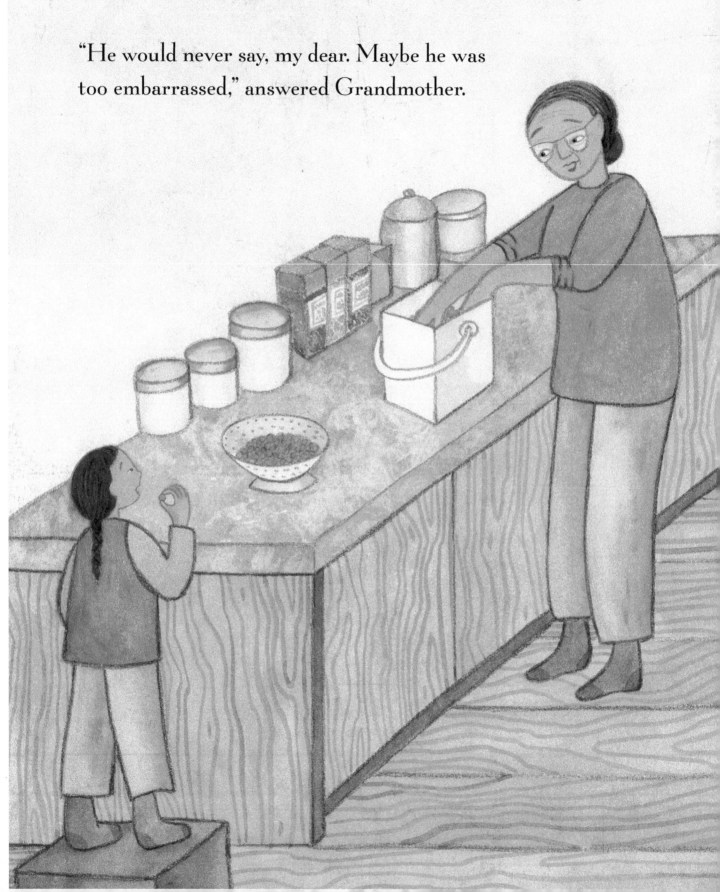

Chulyen noticed the birch tree he sat in. He peeled off a curly piece of bark…

…and placed it where his nose had been. When he really thought about it, Chulyen *did* know where his nose was.

Even though he often acted silly, Chulyen had a way of knowing things.

HE HAD SPECIAL POWERS.

Yes, he knew where his nose was. But how would he get it back?

The bubbling creek below Chulyen flowed into a lake. A small village was nestled on the hillside above it.

While Chulyen was thinking, a *Chida* from the village walked to the beach to gather driftwood for her fire. As she reached for a piece of wood, she noticed something.

Chida (CHEE da): old woman

Brushing off the sand, she examined Chulyen's nose.

Yada di (ya da DEE)

And so she tucked it into her *ulkesa*.

ulkesa (ul KEE suh): sewing bag

She used it to clean the sides of a bowl of *nivagi*, her favorite dessert.

nivagi (ni VAH gi)

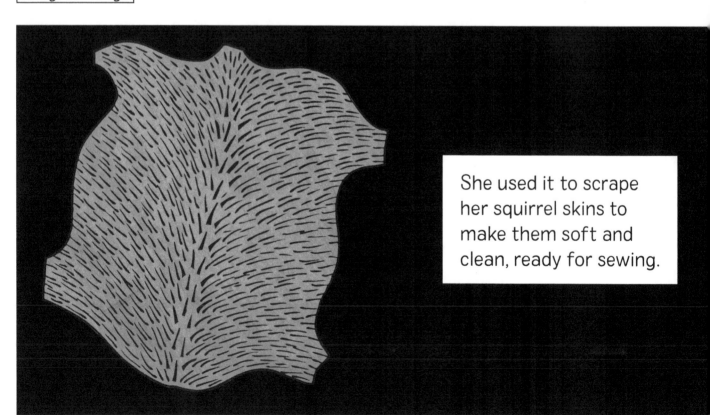

She used it to scrape her squirrel skins to make them soft and clean, ready for sewing.

She used it to take the scales off salmon before she filleted them.

Yes, Chulyen's nose was a wonderful tool.

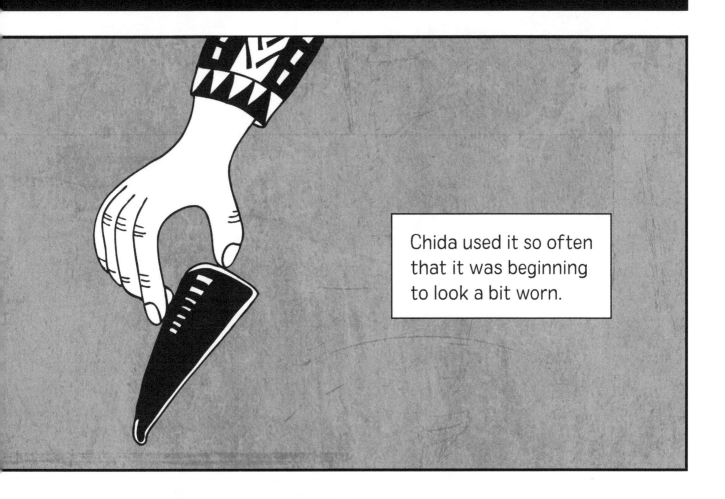

Chida used it so often that it was beginning to look a bit worn.

"What else can Chulyen do?" asked Granddaughter.

"You will see," said Grandmother.

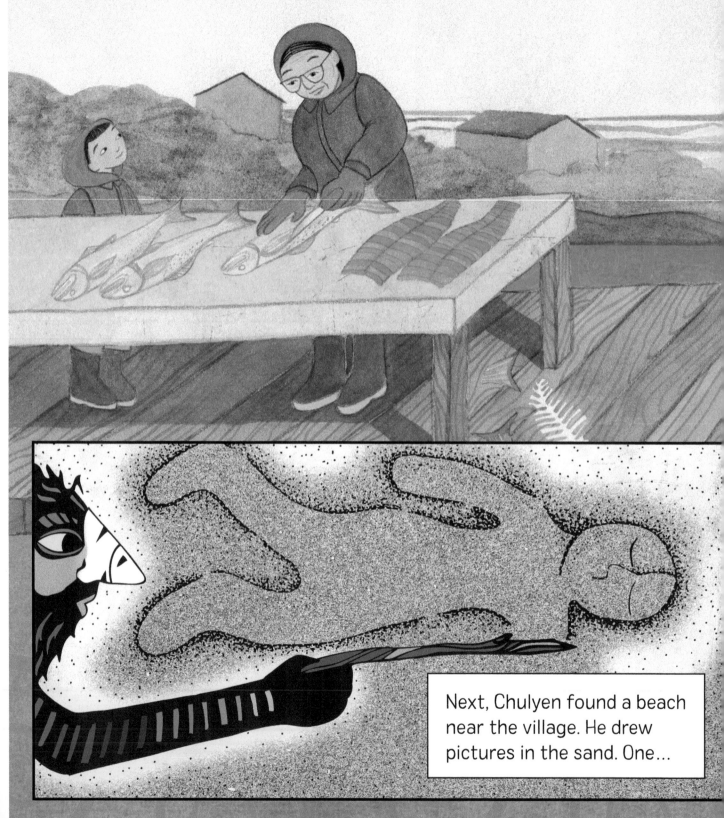

Next, Chulyen found a beach near the village. He drew pictures in the sand. One...

...then another...

...and another...

...and another.

Using his powers, Chulyen spoke to his drawings:

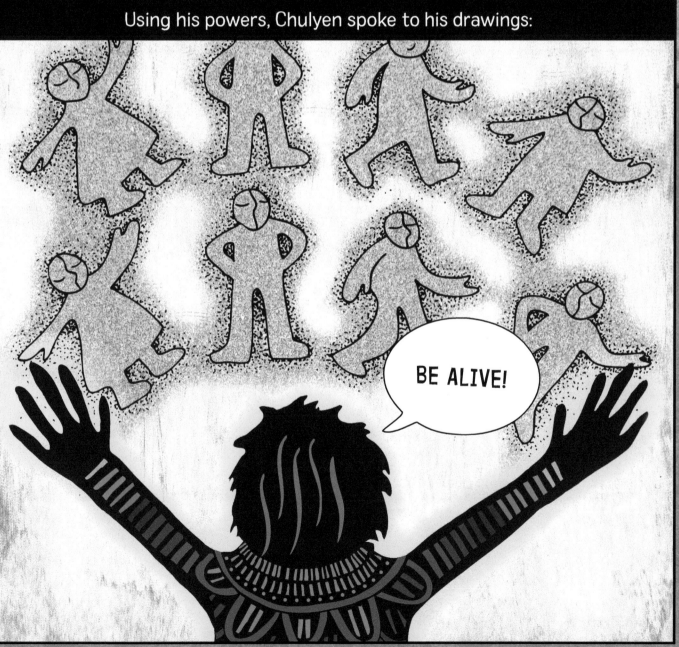

BE ALIVE!

A breeze rippled over the drawings and made them rounded and lifelike.

The group walked toward the village.

MAKE LOTS OF NOISE!

QURR-R-RUK!

QURR-R-RUK!

Chulyen wanted to scare the villagers into running away.

It worked! They did scare the villagers away.

Chida ran away too.

Chulyen knew he did not have much time, for his magic did not last long. His sand drawings would disappear soon and the villagers would return.

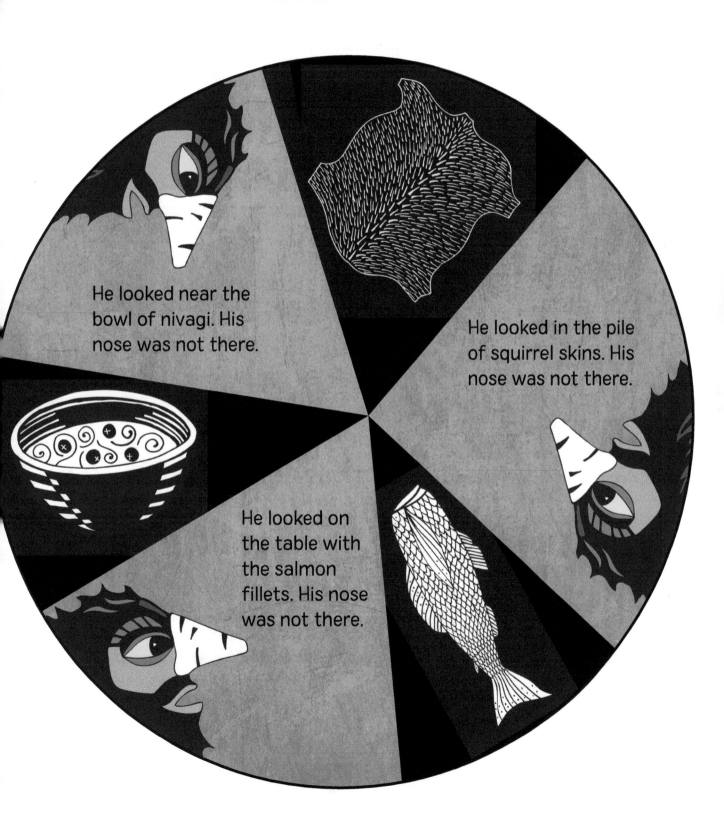

He looked near the bowl of nivagi. His nose was not there.

He looked in the pile of squirrel skins. His nose was not there.

He looked on the table with the salmon fillets. His nose was not there.

As Chulyen rushed around Chida's house...

...his magic began...

...to run out.

Where was his nose?

The villagers were returning. Chida was close.

At last, Chulyen spotted the ulkesa. Inside he found his nose!

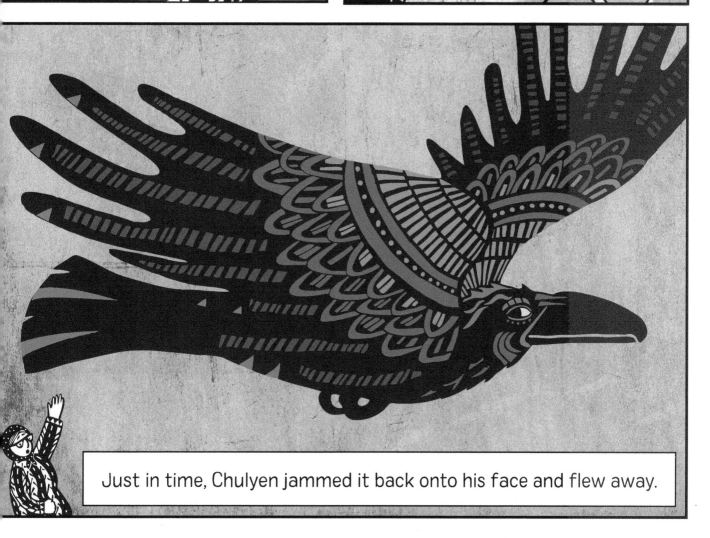

Just in time, Chulyen jammed it back onto his face and flew away.

QURR-R-RUK!
QURR-R-RUK!

Well, Chulyen got his nose back, but if you look carefully you will notice something a little different. It had become soft and worn from Chida's use. Because he was hurrying, Chulyen did not notice. And because of his rush, he jammed it back on without care.

This is why Chulyen has a crooked nose.

"It is always best to take our time and do things right. We may not get a chance to fix our mistakes," said Grandmother. "Just look at Chulyen—he still lives with a crooked nose."

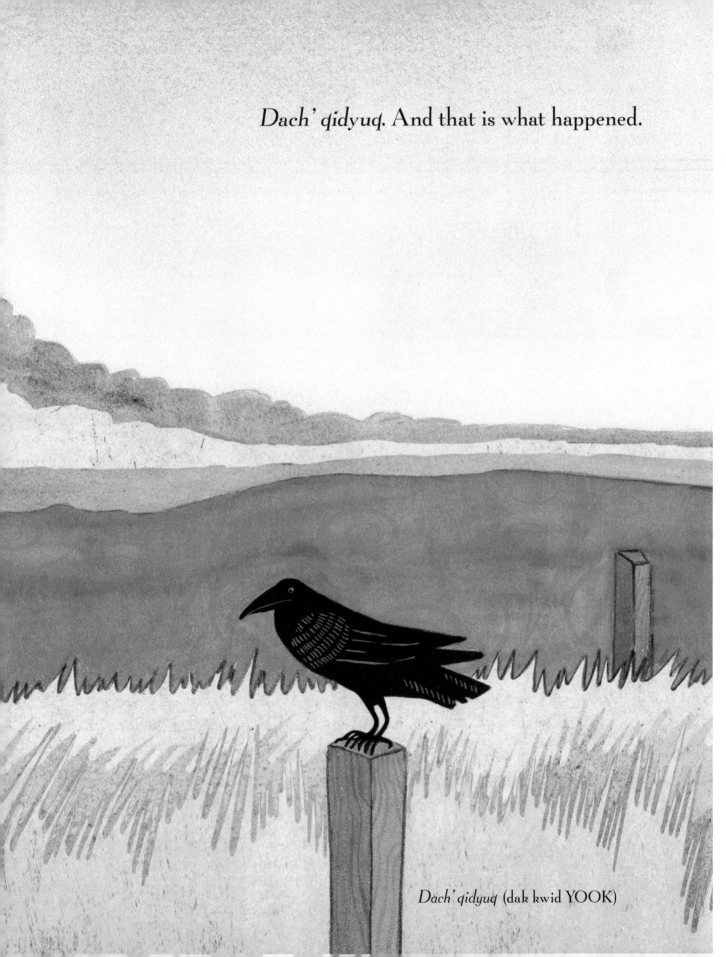

Dach' qidyuq. And that is what happened.

Dach' qidyuq (dak kwid YOOK)

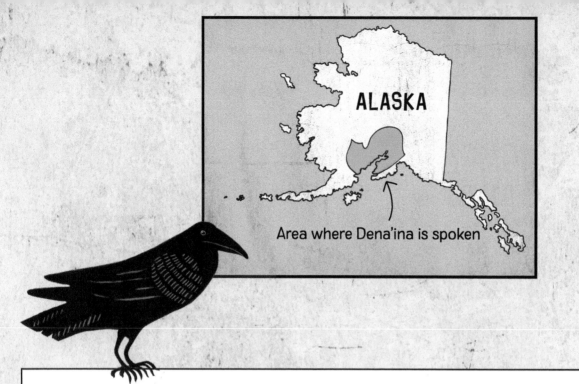

Area where Dena'ina is spoken

MORE ABOUT ALASKAN DENA'INA STORIES

The Dena'ina are an Athabascan language Native people that, to this day, live in the southern part of Alaska, mostly around Cook Inlet. They are the only Athabascan tribe to have migrated and taken up residence at a coastal location.

Their stories were often told to remind or teach their children how to behave. They discuss difficulties the people dealt with. Some are more historic in nature. They all tell something about the culture of the Dena'ina. The story of Chulyen's crooked nose is a teaching story.

Raven, prominent in the Dena'ina story lore as the trickster, often committed naughty and sometimes foolish acts. Like many animals in the Dena'ina stories, he had special powers that enabled him to do fantastical things.

Dena'ina homes were often built on hillsides, away from the shoreline. This made surprise attacks from enemies difficult. Squirrel skins were important to the people. Dena'ina women would climb a nearby mountain in the fall and spend several weeks trapping the arctic ground squirrel, also called the "parka squirrel." They made beautiful, warm blankets and parkas from the skins. Salmon, an essential food of the Dena'ina, was smoked to preserve it. The salmon was made into a kind of jerky that was eaten throughout the winter.

We use Dena'ina words where appropriate to remind us of the Dena'ina origins of the story, or *sukdu*. Dena'ina stories throughout time have ended with *dach' qidyuq*, meaning "and that is what happened..."

Chin'an. Thank you.

Barbara J. Atwater and Ethan J. Atwater
Anchorage, Alaska

DENA'INA GLOSSARY

Chida (CHEE da): grandma or old woman.

Chin'an (chi NUN): thank you.

Chulyen (CHOOL yen): raven.

Dach' qidyuq (dak kwid YOOK): And that is what happened.

K'eduzhizha (kuh ed UZH ee ZHA): Mouth, snout, or beak. The traditional use of "nose" in this story is a personification of the raven.

Nivagi (ni VAH gi): a favorite dish made with a mixture of fresh berries and bound together with a creamed mixture of shortening, sugar, and water or milk.

Sukdu (SOOK du): story.

Ulkesa (ul KEE suh): a small sewing bag that women carried like a purse.

Yada di? (ya da DEE): What is it?

FURTHER READING

Atwater, Barbara J. *Walter's Story; Pedro Bay, Alaska - Past, Present and Distant Memories.* Anchorage: Publication Consultants, 2012.

Johnson, Walter. James Kari, ed. *I'll Tell You a Story (Sukdu Nel Nuheghelnek); Stories I Recall from Growing up on Iliamna Lake.* Fairbanks: Alaska Native Language Center, University of Alaska Fairbanks, 2004.

Jones, Suzi, James A Fall, and Aaron Leggett, eds. *Dena'inaq' Huch'ulyeshi; The Den'ina Way of Living.* Fairbanks: Alaska Native Language Center, University of Alaska Fairbanks, 2013.

Kari, James, ed. *Dena'ina Topical Dictionary.* Fairbanks: Alaska Native Language Center, University of Alaska Fairbanks, 2013.

EDICATION

To our great uncle Walter Johnson who told us many stories, including this one. Whenever he told us a story he would say, "Now you go and tell this story in your own way." We have taken this both as permission and as a directive. *Chin'an*, thank you, Uncle Walter, for sharing this with us. We now share it with others.

This paperback edition ISBN: 9781513264394

Library of Congress Cataloguing-in-Publication Data for the Hardcover

Names: Atwater, Barbara J., author. | Atwater, Ethan J., author. | Dwyer, Mindy, 1957- illustrator.
Title: How raven got his crooked nose : a Dena'ina fable / retold by Barbara J. Atwater and Ethan J. Atwater ; illustrated by Mindy Dwyer.
Description: Berkeley : Graphic Arts Books, [2018] | Audience: Age 5.
Identifiers: LCCN 2017043436 (print) | LCCN 2018005431 (ebook) | ISBN 9781513260969 (ebook) | ISBN 9781513260952 (hardcover)
Subjects: LCSH: Dena'ina Indians--Folklore. | Ravens--Juvenile fiction. | Indians of North America--Alaska--Folklore. | Alaska--Folklore.
Classification: LCC E99.T185 (ebook) | LCC E99.T185 A89 2018 (print) | DDC 398.209798--dc23
LC record available at https://lccn.loc.gov/2017043436

LSI2020

Published by Alaska Northwest Books®
An imprint of

WEST MARGIN PRESS

WestMarginPress.com

WEST MARGIN PRESS
Publishing Director: Jennifer Newens
Marketing Manager: Angela Zbornik
Project Specialist: Gabrielle Maudiere
Editor: Olivia Ngai
Design & Production: Rachel Lopez Metzger

CPSIA information can be obtained
at www.ICGtesting.com
Printed in the USA
JSHW071437260523
42315JS00008B/212

9 781513 264394